Surviving Seventh Grade

Day One

Heather Still

ALSO BY

The Surviving Seventh Grade series:

Sean's Survival Guide
Kayla's Quest (April 2025)
Surviving Seventh Grade: Day One, a prequel novella

Surviving Seventh Grade: Day One

Heather Still

Contents

Title Page   VII

1: Kayla   1

2: Sean   5

3: Kayla   9

4: Sean   16

5: Kayla   21

6: Sean   26

7: Kayla   31

8: Sean   34

9: Kayla   38

10: Sean   44

Want to read more?   46

About the Author   48

An Excerpt from Sean's Survival Guide   49

An Excerpt from Kayla's Quest   56

Surviving Seventh Grade

Day One

Heather Still

1: KAYLA

"Wait!" Mom's voice echoed from inside the house. "I want Max in the picture."

Dad's hand, which was raised to snap a hundred pictures with his phone, dropped to his side. We shared a knowing smile. *Every year.*

"Mom," my older sister Alicia whined, "I need to go. Zach will be here any second." Her voice bounced off the hard stucco walls and brick path of our courtyard.

I couldn't resist mimicking her, ending with my opinion on the whole Zach situation. "Your boyfriend can wait an entire minute for you."

"Please, Kayla. I beg you," Alicia muttered next to me as she straightened her skirt, "grow up." Immaculately dressed as always, Alicia looked like a model for *Seventeen* in her new miniskirt, frilly tank top, flirty half-sweater, and strappy sandals.

Clever comebacks weren't my thing, so I steamed in silence with my arms folded in front of my chest, not at all worried about wrinkling my Rip Curl tank top.

Mom bolted out the front door with our Chihuahua-rat terrier dangling in her outstretched arms. "Hold him," she said, thrusting him at Alicia.

My sister's eyes bulged wide. "I will not." Alicia responded with such horror, Mom might as well have told her she couldn't wear makeup to school.

But Mom didn't blink. "Here," she said to me.

I eagerly accepted her offering. "Hey Maxie-poo." I cradled him like a baby in my arms. His little, warm body squirmed in my grasp. The squirming dog was as much a part of our first day of school picture ritual as the nice clothes and painted on smiles.

But Mom continued to stare at me. "That's what you're wearing for the first day of school?"

"I wanted to wear my new O'Neil shirt, but it's dirty."

Mom looked skyward. I knew the look well. It was her why-can't-you-be-more-like-your-sister look. My sister, who was too worried about getting her clothes dirty to hold our dog, spent thirty-minutes getting dressed for school every day. Thirty-minutes I spent sleeping.

After seven years of dressing up in skirts and dresses for the first day of school, and then never wearing a skirt again the rest of the year, it was time for change.

Actually, it was time for major changes this year. First change: my clothes. I wore a newish surf tank, one I wore most of the summer, with my new turquoise board shorts. If flip-flops were allowed at school, I would have worn those, too. The surfer chick look was so me. I learned how to surf a couple of months ago. I had the best summer ever at surf camp and I wanted to prolong that carefree and fearless feeling throughout the school year.

My second change I planned to enact that morning was recruiting more friends to my group. I even had a specific new friend in mind.

Mom looked at her cell phone. "We still have a few minutes. Can you please go change? Your cute plaid dress is clean and hanging in your closet."

She might as well have slapped me. "Plaid?" That was the opposite of surfer chic.

"Mom," Alicia said, her voice as rough as the stucco wall behind us. "Zach's almost here."

We took our normal positions in the open gate leading through the courtyard to our front door.

"Come on, girls, smile," Dad said, grimacing at the visual he saw from his phone. "This is your last First Day of School picture together."

"I will definitely take a selfie and send it to you from Cal next year," Alicia said.

"Finally, genuine smiles." Dad snapped a couple of pictures.

Alicia and I shared a look, her genuine smile from picturing herself at college and far away from home next year. My genuine smile also from picturing her far away from home next year.

Zach's red Ford truck pulled up in front of the house.

"Gotta go!" Alicia scooped up her backpack and jetted, not looking back.

"Have a great first day," Mom called out as we watched my sister march down the brick path to her boyfriend's truck like a woman on a mission. Alicia was all about seizing every day. *Go big or go home* was her life's motto.

I set Maxie on the cement walk in the courtyard between our front door and the gate leading to the driveway and street. His little legs quickly propelled him back into the house. I followed him inside and took inventory of my backpack for the third time that morning. Even though I probably wouldn't need all my supplies on the first day of school, I wanted to be prepared for all possibilities, which meant a binder with dividers and paper and a full supply pouch with pencils, highlighters, a ruler, colored pencils, a protractor and compass.

The first day of school in middle school was so different from elementary school. Last year was terrifying; the seventh and eighth graders towered over me. Finding each class was a struggle. This year, I knew how to navigate the halls and buildings. This year I knew there were bigger concerns than eighth graders and getting to class. I was a little curious about the teachers and a lot concerned about who was in my class (I *better* have a friend in each class).

Neither of my besties were in any of my classes—not one! Not a good start. Aditi and Thea, being on the college-bound track already, took accelerated classes, which meant they had three classes together. I had straight A's last year, too, but my other best friend and I weren't on the so called "accelerated plan."

"Almost ready?" Mom asked, coming up behind me and peering over my shoulder.

"Almost," I mumbled. I had been ready for the past twenty minutes, but I wasn't *really* ready. Thankfully, Mom was driving me to school instead of having to take the bus for the first day. I ran to the bathroom to brush my hair, just in case I hadn't done it already.

Last year I was a naïve, little sixth-grader. This year I was a seventh-grade surfer chic, calm and battle ready. This year, I knew who the enemy was. More than anything else, I prayed for zero classes with Courtney Crenshaw.

2: SEAN

"Dude," Jeff greeted me, pointing up the street. "You barely made it."

Sure enough, as I walked over to him, the big yellow-orange school bus slowed to a stop at the corner. Not that I would have missed it even if I had arrived a couple minutes later. It would take several minutes to load all the kids, especially with the already teary-eyed parents of sixth graders there. Actually, the parent closest to me, whose eyes were definitely glassy, had seventh grade twin girls plus a little one holding her hand. If Mom wasn't a high school teacher welcoming her own students to her class at that very moment, would she have walked me to the bus stop?

I knew beyond a doubt she would be there, being her extra over-protective self, giving me needless advice. It wasn't the first time I was glad she had 150 other kids to worry about.

Jeff gave me his once over. "I see you dressed up for the occasion."

I ignored his sarcasm and shrugged. "You know, first impressions and all that."

He snort-laughed. Jeff, who normally lived in Dodger t-shirts and jeans, wore a two-toned Hollister tee and khaki shorts. I kind of regretted not wearing shorts, with the sun barely up and the temperature already approaching eighty, but jeans and a white tee with a small Adidas logo were as basic as I could get for the big first day.

My new jeans were stiff, but they covered the laces of my sneakers, unlike all the old pairs I found buried in the back of my closet last weekend. Not one of them covered a sliver of my shoes. Yet another growth spurt wreaked havoc in my closet.

By the curb, the tallest boy at the bus stop, and the meanest seventh grader at our school, shouldered his buddy two feet away from him. I heard his trash talk from my spot on the other end of the cluster. Bobby Jones was already doing what he did best: insulting anyone and everyone. Even his buddy. Yeah, that was how he treated *his friends.*

I knew firsthand how much worse he treated his enemies. Not that I was his enemy. He didn't think that highly of me. I was just an easy target for a lethargic bully.

Bobby was the only reason for my late arrival at the bus stop.

Finally, it was our turn to load onto the bus. Even though we were at the second stop for the lake neighborhood, the bus was already over half full and too warm. In order to sit together, we had to sit a few rows behind the driver.

Right before the doors closed, one last kid ran up the steps and paused at the top to survey his options. He found who he was looking for and was almost past me when he paused for a second.

"Hey," he said with a quick head bob in my direction.

"Hey," I said in return. I found Jeff watching me with raised eyebrows. Yeah, I couldn't remember Elijah Jackson ever saying hi to me last year. "He joined my team over the summer," I explained.

Jeff's eyebrows arched a little higher. "He's that good?"

"Yeah. He's good. He plays both defense and striker, depending on where Coach wants his speed." Elijah was not only the new player on my soccer team, but he was the key player for the team to win more games at the premium club level. "We won a lot of games and two tournaments over the summer."

"Cool," Jeff said. "My team won a tournament, too."

"Yep. I was there, remember?"

"Just reminding you."

Jeff played first base and batted cleanup for his traveling baseball team. I played center midfield for my competitive soccer team. The difference was his team hosted the tournament, so it was local and easy for Mitch and me to go watch the games, while all the tournaments I played in over the summer were all over Southern California and one as far as Bakersfield.

The bus pulled away from the curb with a dozen parents waving from the curb. I pulled out my phone and reviewed the screenshot of my schedule.

"Where do you start?" Jeff asked.

"Math in A-Wing. With Mr. White. He must be new. You?"

"English with Mr. Freedle in C-Wing. At least we have science together."

I nodded. I was just as ecstatic now as I was last week when I learned I had a class with Jeff. Already I couldn't wait for fifth period science. To have a good friend in class was power. For the first time, I would have someone to talk to before and after class, and during down times, and maybe even as a partner. After a torturous sixth grade year, where I learned too late smart kids stuck out in the wrong ways, seventh grade had to be better. My plan to survive seventh grade was simple.

1. Avoid answering the teachers' questions.
2. Blend in.

3: Kayla

First day jitters moshed around in my gut as our car approached the school. Cars filled the lot next to the bus drop off and parents blocked the sidewalk in front of the school.

Mom bit her lower lip as she surveyed the situation from the street as she slowed the car for the red light. "It's a madhouse."

I giggled. "So true."

Mom pulled into the line of cars inching forward to the drop off spot. "You're going to have a good day, right?"

"Absolutely. It's going to be great."

She smiled.

I liked it when Mom looked reassured, so I told her all about my plans for the day. "Thea, Aditi, Marissa, and I are meeting by the big sign so we can walk in together. And Aditi's fourth period class is close to the lunch tables so she can snag our spot from last year. And with some luck, I'll have some other friends in my classes this year. It's going to be great." I crossed my fingers, praying just saying so would make it true.

"So good to hear."

When she stopped in the drop off area, she leaned forward, so I offered her my check for a quick kiss.

"Have a great day, Baby."

"Mom," I said with an eye roll. "Bye!"

Beyond the buses and swarm of parents and kids, my school loomed large with its bright white, stucco two-story buildings. Majestic palm trees planted at specific intervals in front of the buildings set the tone for an organized school setting. On the grass between the front building and the busses, the big electronic sign—which everyone called The Big Sign—welcomed us back.

I had planned to meet my best friends by the sign, but two long lines of well-dressed teachers and students in bright purple shirts blocked my path. They cheered and waved giant purple foam paws. As students hurried between the two lines, the staff and students clapped and cheered, working themselves into an excited frenzy. Black and purple balloons bobbed in the breeze above the gates, with more wrapped around the trunks of palm trees. It was the most enthusiastic show of school spirit ever.

Before walking through the cheering crowd, I spun around and snapped a quick selfie—the palm trees perfectly matched my surfer girl vibe. I would have to post it on snapchat asap. I pocketed my phone and searched for my friends. Tons of parents mingled in front of the gated entrance, but I didn't see my friends.

It would have been nice to meet up with my friends before walking through the entrance. But I was a cool surfer chic who rolled with the waves. The surge of kids swelled around me, practically lifting me up into the stream of kids. As one, we flowed through the gauntlet of screaming kids, spastic foam paws, and smiling adults.

After bobbing along through the gate, I veered off to the side to let the surge flow past me. I pulled out my phone. Aditi had already texted me with her new location.

Just beyond the gate was the main courtyard where most everyone hung out before the morning bell. A tall palm tree with four stone benches forming a square around it marked the center of the area where the most popular eighth graders hung out. I found my besties, Aditi and Thea, waiting for me off to the side of the courtyard.

"Kayla," Thea sang, throwing her arms wide to receive my hug. We hugged and acted like we hadn't seen each other in weeks, even though we went back to school shopping for supplies just last week.

Aditi and I shared a quick side hug before she stepped back to survey my outfit. "Interesting choice."

"Of course." I twirled around as if wearing a cute skirt that would flare out for their admiring gazes instead of my long turquoise board shorts that ended a couple of inches above my knees.

"I don't get it," Thea said with her usual bluntness. "Are you going to the beach after school?"

"Maybe." Planning beach trips after school would be the perfect plan for a surfer chic. I would have to work on that.

But neither Aditi nor Thea looked impressed. Aditi wore her usual school uniform of khaki pants, navy blue polo, and comfortable running shoes. "I'm not the only one who didn't dress up," I pointed out.

Thea, however, wore a smart button-up dress with ruffles running on either side of the buttons. Short puffy sleeves displayed her skinny bronze arms. She pasted her hair tight to her scalp before allowing it to puff out in two perfectly symmetrical mounds that looked like pom-poms. She must have spent thirty minutes just on her hair. She wore cute Converse sneakers like sandals with no socks.

"You look fantastic, The," I told her, trying out a new nickname by dropping the 'a' from her name. We could be

The, Ti, and Kay. Blended it all together: TheTiKay. Or maybe TiTheKay? Ha! Sounds like Teethy Kay.

"Of course," Thea said, responding to my compliment with our go-to response to all compliments. Instead of twirling, as I'd already done that, she swayed from side to side, hands splayed out and her head knocked back as if basking in our adulation. But she quickly relaxed to announce, "I've already seen Chris and Sean."

"Really?" I asked, scanning the crowd for him. "How'd he look?"

Thea looked skyward for the briefest of seconds, but really, she brought it up. "Sean looks taller."

"Of course he looks taller," I said. "He grew like three inches this summer." The packed courtyard filled with clusters of kids bursting with first day excitement and nervous energy. I didn't see Sean, but with the mass of students in the courtyard, he was probably there somewhere. I looked for his best friend, but couldn't find him, either.

Thea turned to face Aditi. "Chris looks as cute as ever."

Somehow Chris earned the "cute" award from Thea. Why Thea approved of Aditi's crush on Chris but not my crush on Sean baffled me. Chris was popular. Every girl had him high on her personal list of the cutest boys in our grade. Cute and friendly Sean Miller flew well below the radar, which was just fine. I couldn't wait to see for myself how much taller he was. We spent several week-long summer surf camps together over the summer, but I hadn't seen him in a few weeks.

"Oh, no," Thea said, whipping back to face me with a frown. "Is he the reason you're dressed like this?"

"No." I scanned the crowd again for him, wondering what he's wearing. "I need to find him." But before we went in search of our crushes, Marissa needed to join us. "Where's Marissa?" I asked.

"She should be here by now," Aditi said, pulling out her cell. She swiped away at her phone. "I just texted her," she said.

Thea and my phones immediately dinged.

While we waited for our friend, we watched the thinning stream of students flow by as the clock sped towards the warning bell. The gauntlet of purple clad students thinned as well.

"Oh, and Courtney Crenshaw arrived like she was the flippin' queen of our school," Thea said with another skyward glance. "She does way too much."

I held a hand to stop whatever else she was about to say. "This is a Courtney-free zone this year."

Aditi nodded in immediate agreement. "I hope she's not in any of my classes."

"Me, too," Thea said.

The last thing I wanted to do the first day of school was waste another second on my backstabbing former friend. Courtney ruined PE and English classes last year. I wasn't about to let her ruin my first moments of seventh grade. "Did you see the newest Ferocious Fae book is coming out soon?" That was the best I could. My forced smile tugged at the corners of my mouth. Courtney wasn't going to bother me at all this year. She no longer existed as far as I was concerned. *She can make all her petty, snide comments she wants about me, because I won't notice her at all.*

She was dead to me.

The warning bell rang.

Aditi brightened. "Time for class. We'll find Marissa at lunch."

Thea and I didn't argue. We left the main courtyard and headed towards the heart of campus, where three two-story buildings, A-Wing, B-Wing, and C-Wing, formed a giant U on one side with the main brick building on the other. We followed hundreds of students heading down the main path between the large buildings. To the left was a smaller courtyard-like space with ten lunch tables and a few small trees in the middle of the U. To the right were the cafeteria lines and windows and a hundred more lunch tables beneath solar panels, which was the main lunch area.

Thea grabbed my upper arm and squeezed with sudden urgency. "Look!"

She pointed at a group of seventh-grade girls breaking a part with loud goodbyes in Spanish and English, with overly dramatic waves, as if they wouldn't see each other for weeks. One girl, the one with her hair pulled tight at the scalp into a long ponytail, looked like Marissa. She was the right height with curly dark brown hair. But the big hoop earrings, deep black eyeliner, and shiny lips did not look like my best friend.

"What's she doing with them?" Aditi asked.

Was it really Marissa? The girl grinned at one of her friends as the two turned towards us and linked elbows. It was Marissa.

"Saying goodbye to her new besties," Thea said in a flat tone.

Did she not see Aditi and Thea waiting by the entrance? Did she not see the text? I headed straight for Marissa. Marissa and her friend veered off towards the front building. "Marissa!" I called out.

Marissa barely glanced over, just enough to see me, before turning around and walking away with the other girl.

My feet turned to stone. I stopped in the middle of the hallway. "What just happened?" I looked at my friends with my palms raised helplessly.

"It's a defection," Thea said with a frown.

Marissa linked elbows with the girl next to her as they walked, as if completely unaware that she just straight up ignored me and my friends.

"Not cool," was all I said, fighting to hide the hurt. Already I was starting the year with a negative. Minus one best friend.

4: Sean

My friend Mitch and I parted from Jeff as he went to his class past the lunch area and we stayed by the main courtyard area. Students lined up in long lines by the classroom doors to lower-level classrooms outside and soon Mitch joined a line downstairs. I continued upstairs to my second-floor math class, feeling more like sheep being herded to class.

The identical buildings all had an outdoor hallway bisecting the second floor, with doors to classrooms every 40 feet on both sides of the hallway. This made the hallways packed with lines of students against the walls and swarms of students heading in each direction in the middle. No one paid any attention to the directions painted on the ground, even on the first day when everyone was on their best behavior.

I joined the line of students waiting to shake hands with our teacher before being admitted into class. I leaned against the stucco wall, the dull tips of plaster worn down from years of students just like me leaning against it.

Was there anything worse than math first thing in the morning? Well, besides PE first thing in the morning, which I knew firsthand from last year.

I shuffled along towards the front of the line, getting a better view of my math teacher who towered over the students. He was so tall, he must have been a college basketball player, and not too long ago. Mr. White had a stubbly goatee, close cut black hair, and a snazzy light gray, three-piece suit. He easily won the best-dressed teacher award.

When it was my turn to shake hands with the new math teacher, he gave me a brilliant smile with perfectly white teeth, and said, "Hey, I'm Mr. White," with a cool, at ease, and very confident vibe.

I couldn't help but return his grin as I shook his hand. "I'm Sean Miller."

His eyes lit up. "No way, *you're* Sean Miller?" He chuckled with glee. "I saw you on my roster. Awesome. Your mom was my favorite teacher."

And there went the perfectly good start to the school year. The bell hadn't rung yet and he already labeled me a teacher's kid. Not just any teacher's kid, but Mom's kid.

"Mrs. Miller is one of my *whys*." When all I could do was stare at him blankly, he added, "*Why* I'm a teacher."

"Oh, cool." Not sure if I could slip inside the classroom or not, I continued standing there, stiff and awkward, with my thumbs tucked under the straps to my backpack.

"She used to talk about you all the time. Do you still play soccer?"

"Oh, uh, yeah." Oh wow. He must have just graduated from college. I had been playing soccer for six or seven years max.

"Cool, cool. Well, you're in front. Find your name on the table."

Great. I ducked into the classroom, already dreading the class. Instead of the traditional, orderly rows of desks, the classroom had single desks and chairs clustered in groups of three crammed into the main part of the classroom. The blank, empty walls were in stark contrast to the chaotic cluster of desks. But even in the organized chaos setup, my seat was front and center and just where a tall, skinny boy wanted to sit. Said no tall, skinny boy ever.

I dropped my backpack on the desk with my name on it and slid into the creaky plastic chair connected to it. Another stark contrast to the empty walls was the one big window, its view almost entirely of green palm fronds.

The name on the sticky note for the desk next to me added dead weight to the dread in the pit of my gut: Bobby Jones.

Sure enough, before I could do anything about it, the big, mean dude slumped into the seat next to me.

"Miller," he greeted with a sneer.

I forced out a meek, "Bobby." My eyes fled from his glare. I watched my math teacher, noting every step and every smile, as if my life depended on it.

With my legs stretched out half a mile from my desk, I worried Mr. White might trip over them as he strolled back and forth in the front of the class with a stack of syllabuses forgotten in his hand. Mr. White clearly had too much coffee that morning. I crossed my arms on the desk in front of my chest and slumped another inch or two deeper into my chair, trying to get as low as possible so that maybe no one would notice me.

The tiny girl next to me, so tiny I thought she was a sister of a student when I saw her outside, sat up as tall as possible with hands folded on the desk. She wore a Barbie pink and black argyle vest with matching knee socks and reminded me of an anime character. While my size twelve Adidas Sambas created a walking hazard for Mr. White, her fancy heels didn't touch the floor. This summed up middle school perfectly. We should have our own comic strip.

While Mr. White continued to talk about what was probably on the paper he forgot to hand out, I pulled out my spiral notebook. I leaned over my desk to block Bobby from seeing my idea for a middle school comic, featuring me, Super-Sized Sean, and the tiniest seventh grader in the world. I named her Teeny Tiny Tina.

Done with my sketches, I next worked hard on some clever dialogue with Teeny Tiny Tina giving Super-Sized Sean some sage advice on surviving the first day of seventh grade. It was at this point when Mr. White realized he was still holding his precious syllabus. He glided down the aisles like a basketball player running drills, handing a set of papers to one student, then swiveling to hand out papers to another student on the other side, then gliding two steps forward to repeat the moves in a graceful rhythm.

When the bell rang, which was not a surprise at all since I had been tracking the minute hand for the last ten minutes, I jammed my syllabus and notebook into my backpack. I bounded for the door, needing to put as much distance as possible between Bobby and me, and was halfway to the door when someone called my name.

My head swiveled around, but my body continued toward the door, not wanting to allow Bobby to catch up. There, in the back of the mass exodus, Elijah stood with his half wave, half salute. Oh.

I stopped and scurried back to let the escapees sweep past. Bobby bounded past me without a second glance.

"Hey," I said to Elijah when he joined me.

"Hey." Again he gave me a half nod. Elijah wasn't a guy who did anything halfway, besides gestures. Like a lot of the boys, he wore dark jeans with trendy little rips around a knee and opposite thigh, along with the newest Air Jordans. "Sucks, you're stuck in front."

"No kidding. I thought for sure the teacher was going to trip over me."

He busted out with a loud laugh. "Right?" We left class and continued to walk together down the stairs. "I can't believe he didn't trip over those colossal feet of yours."

"Colossal?" Sure, they were big, but I was "growing into them," as Mom said, and they were awesome for soccer.

"It's my favorite roller coaster right now. Nothing's huge anymore. Everything's *colossal*." Elijah flashed his bright white teeth in a big, cheesy grin. "Mr. White seems cool," he said, switching topics with *colossal* speed. "I'm glad we have him instead of Mr. Grimly."

"Yeah." As we walked past the courtyard area, tons of kids waved or called to Elijah as we walked by. I never walked next to someone whom so many kids wanted to say "Hi" to before. It was like walking with a celebrity.

Despite Bobby Jones and my horrible seat, math might be my favorite class.

5: Kayla

It was easy to find Aditi and Thea in the mass of kid-covered tables. It was the same spot as last year.

"Sweet," I said as I plunked down next to Aditi. "This is the best part of my day by far." I pulled out my lunch bag from my backpack, glad to not have to stand in the long line for food on my first day back.

"I am so hungry," Aditi said, gazing at her little piles of food set just so in her container from home.

"Kayla, you know Janae, right?" Thea asked me with a head bob towards the girl next to her.

"Oh, awesome, hi!" The girl gave me a small, shy smile. "We had PE together last year, right?"

Janae smiled and nodded, but didn't say anything, which was exactly what I remembered about her. She was nice, but really quiet. She had a killer sense of style, though, pairing a cute dress with Doc Marten combat boots, and her silky, almost black hair in two expertly done French braids.

"And I'm Brit," the girl on the other side of Aditi said, leaning past my bestie so we could see each other. She had long, shiny brown hair and dark brown eyes, and I was 90% positive I had never seen her before.

"Hi, Brit." Aditi and Thea recruited more friends! Brilliant. Brit wore a cute plaid mini skirt (plaid!), shiny lip gloss, and glittery lavender eyeshadow. While her look was far from my new surfer look, she could definitely hang with the social snobs of our school.

The best and most important thing: Brit and Janae filled Marissa's empty spot.

"Are you new?" I asked Brit.

"Sure am," she said with another friendly smile.

"Cool. Where are you from?"

"San Diego area. Escondido. My dad got some big promotion and got transferred to the office here. It's a bummer having to move. I miss my friends so much, but the boys here are so *cute*."

Giggles and some disbelief followed.

"Our boys are cuter than your boys?" Thea asked, her high arched brows saying more than her disbelieving tone.

"So cute," Brit said.

"See," I said, almost sticking my tongue out at my besties. "I told you. I bet Brit will agree with me that Sean's cute." I pointed at a table towards the back corner. "He's the tall blond boy in the white shirt. Isn't he cute?"

Brit's eyes sparkled and her lips, all pink and shimmery from lip gloss, curved into an open, excited smile. "Totally," she agreed, even as her eyes searched for him. Like Marissa, Brit wore thick black mascara that framed her brown eyes. She looked good, not like a clown or anything, but she definitely wore a ton more makeup than Thea, Aditi and me combined, which was, well, none.

On second thought... "But he's mine—or at least, he will be mine. Soon."

Her eyes lit up. "Ooh, sounds juicy. Dish!"

I shrugged, pretending I didn't have a plan.

But Brit, unfazed, launched into a long rundown of all the cute boys she met so far. She didn't mention Sean, but she didn't know most of the boys' names and had to describe them. Our new friend Brit was the most boy crazy girl ever. What a great addition to our group!

The bell rang. Aditi sprang to her feet in excitement and Thea said, "Finally. Math class!"

Brit and I both groaned at the same time, then shared a smile. Already, Brit naturally moved into Marissa's spot, joining me in our polar opposite responses to my besties.

"What do you have now?" I asked Brit.

"English," she muttered with an eye roll. "You?"

"Science," I said with equal dread.

My besties and Janae bailed, with Brit and I trudging after them. I enjoyed talking about boys with Brit. Thea and Aditi mostly shrugged or rolled their eyes when I talked about Sean. They didn't have to say it out loud; I knew they were shocked to discover someone even more gaga over boys than me. In my defense, I was only crazy about one boy. Brit was the one who looked around the lunch area like a child given a hundred dollars to spend in a candy shop.

All my friends turned in one direction while I headed to my science class in the C Wing. So far I had zero good friends in any of my classes. It looked like it would be another year of having to make friends in all my classes, which was how I met both Aditi and Thea last year, but still...

All the teachers made us line up outside the classroom and enter one at a time, often where we had to shake their hands or exchange polite greetings. By fifth period, the routine was staler than croutons. Except...as I walked past the kids in the line for my class, the day exploded to the top of the list of best days ever.

Right in front of me, in the middle of the line of students waiting to enter the classroom, was none other than Sean Miller! Oh, he was so cute, just standing there, wearing his backpack with his hands shoved into his jeans pockets, talking with the boy next to him.

"Hi Sean," I said, my shocked but excited tone legit. "It's so cool you have Ms. Woodson, too."

When his green eyes met mine, I almost melted from that warm and friendly gaze of his. The corners of his mouth immediately curved up in a smile. "Hi Kayla."

Just like that, he returned my greeting, matching my sheer joy at seeing him with his own friendly smile.

"I'm so glad you're in this class," I said and stepped a little closer to join him. "You're my only friend so far."

Whatever his green eyes hadn't melted, his lazy grin would finish cooking into a puddle.

"Yeah, this is great." He looked from me to his best friend, Jeff Grayson. Jeff, Sean, and I all went to the same elementary school, so we went way back. But I hadn't really talked to Sean until last summer at surf camp. Sean had always been a cute boy, and one of the nicer ones, too, but it wasn't until last summer when I started majorly crushing on him.

Wanting to remind him of how much fun we had together over the summer, I picked the obvious question. "Have you been surfing lately?"

"Of course," he said with an easy smile. "I went yesterday with my dad."

"Nice."

"And you?"

"Oh, well, not since camp, no. But I hope to go soon."
My mind went to my crazy plan to go surfing after school
sometime soon. Should I ask him to go with me?

Before I could decide, he turned to look past Jeff, dis-
tracted by someone at the end of the line.

As a cheery, confident person, there wasn't much that
could turn an amazing sunny day into a dreary, stormy one.
Equally true, there weren't too many people that made my
stomach shudder and turned my feet to heavy cement so
that I stood there, petrified. In fact, there was only one
person in the world who could do that, and she had the
nerve to join the end of the line for my science class.

Invisible clouds hovered overhead, dropping me into
the shadows of dread. At the end of the line stood Courtney Crenshaw.

6: SEAN

I HADN'T EVEN ENTERED the classroom yet and science was already the best class. Jeff and I stood in line outside our science class, talking with my friend Kayla from surf camp. While we knew each other from elementary school, we became something like friends hanging out in surf camp last summer. Judging by the way she smiled and headed straight for me, the friendship we started in camp could continue in school. It would be nice to have a friend who was a girl.

Kayla tossed her hair back over a tanned shoulder that told her story of a summer spent at the beach. I also spent my summer in the sun, between the beach and the soccer field, but my skin only burned and peeled, with no tan. As I envied her golden tan, the one and only Courtney Crenshaw flashed past me in a bright pink dress.

Shock jolted through me. I whipped around to see if she joined my class's line. No way was she in my class. I already hit the jackpot with both Jeff and Kayla in my class. I didn't have the sort of luck that would allow the girl I crushed on last year to be in my science class.

And yet, somehow, she stopped at the end of our line.

Courtney looked like a modern-day Disney princess in her delicate pink sundress, with her hair done up in a loose knot with wispy curls framing her face. I looked around, wondering what happened to the cartoon birds that should circle around her.

Too late, I noticed the silence. I swiveled back around, frantically trying to remember what we were talking about seconds ago.

Kayla stared back at the end of the line, too.

Jeff wasn't any help. He stood on his tiptoes, looking behind us, trying to figure out what caught both Kayla and my attention.

Before I could think of a clever distraction to pull my friends away from staring at my crush, the science teacher, Ms. Woodson, stepped out of the open door.

"Welcome class," she greeted in a loud, carrying voice. Seconds later, the line surged forward.

When it was time for me to introduce myself to my teacher, she greeted me with a friendly smile.

"Ah, Sean, welcome to class." Ms. Woodson scanned the clipboard in her hand. Unlike Mr. Smith, my science teacher wore black pants that were like jeans, but weren't jeans. She had a simple button up blouse, and I got the feeling that's how she'd dress the rest of the year. Also, unlike Mr. Smith, Ms. Woodson had been teaching at our school for a really long time. "You're in seat B1." She flashed me a fast, enthusiastic smile, as if exhausting all her stored energy on this one action, like a flight attendant going through the safety procedures for the thousandth time.

I nodded and ducked into class, hoping the information she gave me made sense when I got inside.

It was a science class like all other science classes at the school, with tables in the front and middle of the class and large black lab counters around the perimeter. Hanging from the ceiling above were lime green, laminated rectangles, each with a large black letter that mapped out a grid. I walked to the opposite side of the classroom, found the number one in the second row, pulled the chair out from under the desk with a loud screech of metal against the hard floor, and plunked down in the plastic chair.

Jeff and Kayla hurried in behind me and followed me all the way to the seats right behind me.

Kayla beamed at me and everyone who walked by. "This is perfect," she said. "I've never sat with friends in class before."

"Yeah," I said. It was a first for me, too.

I sat sideways in my chair to talk freely with Jeff and Kayla while people streamed into class and sat down. Courtney walked in ten kids later and drifted to the back of the class on the opposite side of the room. When she sat down, she disappeared behind all the kids seated between us.

Once everyone sat down and long after the tardy bell rang, Ms. Woodson greeted the class.

"Welcome to seventh grade science," she said, stepping past the large, dark Promethean board that looked like it was out-of-place in the middle of the classroom. She gave the class another smile and opened her mouth to speak again, but then stopped. "Yes?"

"Ms. Woodson," a girl's voice sang out from the recesses of the classroom. "My glasses broke and I can't see you. Can I move up to the front?"

"Oh," our teacher said, appearing a little startled by the request. She glanced at the row directly in front of her and suddenly everyone was staring at the empty seat next to Aurora. "Good for you for speaking up and advocating for yourself. Please move to this seat."

"Thank you," the syrupy sweet voice said. Courtney gracefully stood with her backpack and hurried to the front of the class to join her best friend.

Behind me, Kayla grumbled, "Broken glasses, yeah, right."

Courtney wearing glasses was as likely as me jumping up and serenading the class with an Ed Sheeren song, but I appreciated Courtney's clever play.

Who knows how long I envisioned myself singing a totally awesome rendition of "Perfect" to Courtney with the class clapping and snapping to the beat, but eventually I returned to reality and discovered Ms. Woodson had asked the class a question. The first of many questions she would ask us throughout the year, and the first of many I wouldn't volunteer an answer. It helped not hearing the question.

When no one raised their hand, Ms. Woodson looked at her seating chart. "Kayla?" she said with eyebrows quirking up a smidge.

"Oh, um, yeah. Let's see...Last year in science, I remember...doing lab experiments...?"

"Yes, I would hope so," our teacher said. "Which experiments?"

Her blue eyes grew dark with the panic that struck when thirty-three pairs of eyes watched in riveted fascination.

Not cool on the first day.

Against my will, my stupid hand shot up, the motion more of a reflex, like reaching out to catch a ball when it's thrown at me.

"Yes-" she looked down at her chart again, "-Sean?"

I rattled off a few things that came to mind. "We did a lab with Alka Seltzer tablets, used microscopes, adopted and tracked the recovery of a rescued marine mammal, and learned to use scratch for projects."

"Excellent, Sean." Ms. Woodson beamed at me.

"Tryhard," some kid coughed out in the back.

Of course he did. Last year I heard that insult coughed from the back of the classroom more times than I cared to remember.

Behind me Kayla whipped around to fire back at the kid, "That was so last year."

Next to her, Jeff shook his head at me, knowing how much I didn't want to be *that* kid again. But when Kayla turned back around after her stare down with my attacker, the darkness evaporated from Kayla's eyes. Now her eyes danced and her lips curved up in a big smile.

Her smile was contagious. Sure, I might have set myself up for another year of snide comments, but if it made Kayla that happy, maybe my sacrifice was worth it?

Then a silky, teasing voice said, "Ah, he's just a simp. How cute." Except *simp* sounded nerdy and cute sounded *dirty*.

My face burned hotter than if I'd stuck it in the heart of a bonfire as a couple of kids snickered at the dig. The crushing comment came from none other than Courtney. Her quip that I wasn't so much a *tryhard* as I was crushing on Kayla stung like someone slapping my sunburned back. It was uncomfortable, but not really painful.

"Courtney?" Ms. Woodson pivoted seamlessly. "What do you remember from science last year?"

Straightening her shoulders and tossing her red hair over a shoulder, Courtney answered in a proud, carrying voice, "We went on a field trip." A few more giggles followed.

This was a perfect example of why middle school sucked. Both Courtney and I answered the teacher's questions, but kids labeled me a *tryhard* for helping a friend, while the same kids giggled at Courtney's basic answer. There should be a legit survival guide on the social and political norms of seventh grade.

7: Kayla

Sean Miller saved me!

Why I couldn't think of a single experiment from last year was a frustrating mystery, but in the end, I was glad I couldn't. If I had a decent answer, Sean never would have come to my rescue. Even Courtney, who rarely noticed anyone outside her super selective friend circle, noticed his heroic act. Calling him a *simp* wasn't the nicest way to do it, but since Courtney put the "me" in mean, nice wasn't her thing.

Unfortunately, his furious blush lingered for many minutes. The cause of his blush was up for debate. Maybe her veiled insult embarrassed him. Maybe having thirty plus kids watch him with an odd combination of mocking glee and sympathy did it. Or maybe knowing Courtney noticed him was enough. Any of the reasons, or all of them, could have caused his red cheeks.

While I didn't know Sean nearly as well as I wanted to, after spending many days at the beach with him last summer, I knew a few of his dislikes. He hated sand in his backpack, injuries that kept him from surfing or playing soccer, and kids teasing him in class.

I found out this last one the hard way. The first day of surf camp, I made the mistake of teasing him about his thorough answers in math class last year. He was very smart and wasn't afraid to show it. I admired him for it, but he didn't take it as the compliment I meant it to be.

In fact, he clearly stated that he would not "willingly answer a single teacher's question" this year. And yet, on day one of seventh grade, he already broke his vow. For me!

I needed to thank him. I had to let him know how much I appreciated what he did. If I didn't, I worried he would never do it again. But he didn't turn around the rest of the period.

Which left me alternating between staring at his back, faking interest in whatever Ms. Woodson droned on about, and breaking those two activities up with occasionally doodling on Jeff's planner.

As soon as I finished drawing a blooming rose in the bottom corner of Jeff's weekly planner page, he added a few lines and more circles, turning it into an exploding rose.

"Hey," I whispered, faking offense. I drew a frowning stick figure next to his exploding rose.

Jeff glanced over his shoulder at me as he leaned over to block my view of his planner. Seconds later, he moved back in his seat to reveal a very deranged looking stick figure holding an exploded rose. It reminded me of charred Wiley Coyote holding an exploded present in his hand.

I giggled at the similarities. The silence that followed my giggle made me glance up at our teacher, whose stare might as well have been Superman's laser vision because it left me feeling as burned as the cartoon coyote.

Busted.

Heat trickled up my neck, lashing out at my cheeks. I continued to stare at my teacher. What were the chances Sean would dash to my rescue again? From the lack of response, he appeared to be the only one in class not aware of the showdown between my new science teacher and me. Was it her move or mine?

As the unwanted classroom chess match continued, Sean twisted around in his chair to look back at me. Now the entire class watched.

Why did teachers do this? And on the first day?

I took a deep breath, ready to get the attention off me and onto someone else. I couldn't think of anything brilliant to say, so I asked the first question I thought of.

"Do we have homework?"

Ms. Woodson signed. "No, Kayla, we don't. Not today, at least." She turned her attention back to the entire class and picked up right where she left off, which was apparently discussing late work.

Several long minutes later, when Ms. Woodson was on the opposite side of the classroom helping a student open a backpack, Sean turned back to Jeff and me.

In a low voice just over a whisper, he said, "People say she's the toughest teacher here. Big on due dates. Harsh on late work. Don't even think about being tardy."

I groaned. "Great. She already knows my name."

Jeff snickered next to me. "Better you than me."

Sean's smile of empathy was a pleasant contrast to Jeff's smirk. I smiled back at him before adding to Jeff's planner, giving Jeff's deranged stick figure devil horns.

8: SEAN

ONE DAY. LESS THAN one day was all it took for me to blow my vow to bits. I couldn't even make it six periods without announcing myself to the class as a teacher-pleaser. And to do it in the one class Courtney Crenshaw was in. Unforgiveable.

The only positive was, thanks to Courtney, people believed I was a simp trying to please Kayla, and not the teacher. Which was kind of what happened, but the last thing I wanted was for the entire class to notice me and judge my actions. It was like Courtney's comment shone a spotlight on me for some solo I had not volunteered for.

Hopefully, there was a Do Over option for the first day of school. From this point forward, no more volunteering answers.

While Ms. Woodson continued to talk about expectations, I opened up my planner to the front section, where it walked students through the process of making SMART goals. It looked like a lot of effort, but desperation urged me to scrawl my goal across the top page. It was a simple enough goal. Maybe I needed to set up a reward system for each day I succeed, and then each week, and then each month...

The bell rang.

I glanced up from my planner, checking the clock, not believing the class was already over. All around me kids bounced to their feet, some with backpacks already on, like they had been counting down the seconds until they could escape. Those few jetted out the door, leaving the rest of us unprepared students to shovel our binders, planners, and pencil bags into our backpacks.

Kayla and Jeff both stood next to my desk, chatting about some *deranged monster* (I had no idea why) while I finished packing up.

We walked away from class through the courtyard of the A-wing before I broke off towards the B-wing and then continued on towards the center of campus.

I slipped into my last class early enough to snag a seat in the back row. Finally, a teacher who didn't force assigned seats!

I continued to doodle in my planner, scratching it up with triangles and cubes as students filled the room. With my absolutely stellar luck, Bobby Jones, the unpleasant kid from my bus stop and math class, sauntered in with another large kid like they were linebackers for the school football team. Except we didn't have a school football team.

His buddy took the last open seat that wasn't in the front. Bobby sent his friend a ferocious frown as he slumped low in one of the front row seats.

Seconds later our teacher welcomed the class and launched into a surprisingly entertaining google slide presentation of his vacation pictures intermingling with Xbox winner charts. He was an e-sport competitor with serious credentials. I didn't know teachers could enter e-sport competitions, but I guess it made sense. Why ban teachers but allow everyone else?

Next, Mr. Reynolds covered his class expectations by having us share typical expectations of classes at Central Valley Middle School and then he agreed to all of them. We created tent cards with our names and favorite sports and subjects and even shared a highlight of the summer vacation. I don't know if I've ever talked so much with kids in my class on the first day before I learned that the kid next to me spent a month in Mexico where it was *hotter than Mars*—his words, not mine. The girl on my other side went to Wild Rivers, the water park twenty minutes up the 5 freeway, twice a week all summer. Since they shared fairly normal stuff, I felt comfortable sharing about surf camp.

"How long have you surfed?" the boy asked.

"I started going to surf camp the first summer I was old enough, so about four years now. Have you ever been?"

The boy shook his head, as did the girl.

"I wish," the girl said in awe. "I gotta learn to swim first."

"Uh, yeah. That's probably best."

How could someone live in Central Valley and not know how to swim? I congratulated myself for not showing my shock. There were several beaches not thirty minutes from school. Plus, there were four rec centers with pools and the Central Valley Lake all in Central Valley. She must have worked hard at not knowing how to swim.

Our teacher rang a chime, and the class grew quiet.

"Would anyone like to share with the whole class?"

A few brave souls raised their hands. I was dismayed to find my hand betrayed me by shooting straight up in the air.

"Yes..." she said as she glanced at my tent card, "...Sean?"

I took a quick breath before sharing in a strong, carrying voice, "I went to surf camp for a few weeks."

My teacher's eyebrows shot up. "Surf camp? For a few weeks? Fun."

"Me, too," another boy chimed in from the row ahead of me. He turned back to look at me. "Which one did you go to?"

I checked with the teacher to make sure I could answer. He nodded encouragingly, so I did.

The boy went to a different surf camp, one in San Diego near a hotel his family stayed at, while I went to a local one. But it was cool to learn there was another kid in my class who not only surfed, but went to surf camp. For some reason, surf camp wasn't nearly as popular as it should be.

Even better, kids in the class thought surf camp was cool, even if they had never heard of it before. Maybe volunteering and answering questions in class wasn't the worst thing to do after all.

9: KAYLA

SCIENCE WAS THE BEST class ever. I wanted to bust out my phone and text my friends the moment I sat down in history class, but everyone knew my teacher was extra strict, so I had to wait. I mentally composed my text over and over during the first few minutes of my last class.

My history teacher smiled a little and scowled a lot, which wasn't ideal. She also listed the topics we were going to learn about that year like she was a server reading an entire menu to us.

But then she started going into greater detail about the projects and activities we would do, projects like google slides, creating podcasts, and maintaining a digital portfolio. For the first time, project-based learning sounded cool. While she wasn't chill and fun like Mr. White, nor a little goofy like Ms. Woodson, my history teacher described super creative projects, and I loved being creative.

When she finished explaining the class, she had us number off and move around the room. I stood in the corner near the door with three kids I didn't know. There, we followed her instructions and introduced ourselves and our favorite food. Then we created a group celebration—High Ten, Y'all—and practiced until we were told to stop.

Our teacher then explained, "Now, when I ask a question, the first group to all raise their hands gets to answer the question. If you answer correctly, the entire class does the group's celebration, and the group gets a point. If you answer incorrectly, the other groups will politely clap, but no point for you."

I had never heard of a game like it, but as I already figured out, my history teacher was creative. It was the best game ever. The goofier the celebration, the better. We didn't care that she was asking us questions about the syllabus she just covered. We didn't care if the other team got more points. All we cared about was someone getting the answer right so we could loudly and wildly celebrate.

Once the game ended and we returend to our seats, the boy next to me said, "Can we play again tomorrow?"

He earned the first proper smile from our teacher.

I left my history class with a smile almost as bright as when I walked out of science with Sean and Jeff. As I headed for the buses, I kept an eye out for my besties and Sean, but I also stayed alert to any others I wanted to avoid (*others* being Courtney).

Marissa, my absent friend from the morning, wound up walking right in front of me as hundreds of students headed for the front of the school. Her gigantic silver hoops swung from her earlobes as she tossed her head back and forth, loudly laughing at whatever the girl next to her said. She looked nothing like my friend Marissa from last year. Still, I had to try.

"Marissa!" I shouted.

Her shoulders jumped before she spun around.

"Kay! You scared the crap out of me!" Except she didn't say crap, and instead said a Spanish word that probably meant something a little harsher than crap.

I wasn't about to apologize. "What's up with ditching us?"

Marissa frowned and looked at her friend before glaring at all the kids parting and rushing past us on either side. "Do we have to do this now? *Here?*"

With hands on hips, I assumed my Wonder Woman stance. "Yes." I needed answers.

Both of her hands flew up to straighten her ponytail, and then her fingers pressed any stray hairs flat against her scalp. "Fine." One more look at her friend, then she gave me her full attention. "I'm tired of taking a backseat to perfect Aditi and amazing Thea. I'm done with always doing what they want to do. Aren't you?"

"No," I said immediately. "They're super smart and do great things. What's wrong with that?"

She gave me a pitying look before turning to her friend as if to say *see*. "Whatever Kayla. You do you. I have new friends."

Then she turned her back to me, linked her elbows with her new best friend, and walked away.

I rode the bus home that day, and for the entire ride I texted Aditi and Thea, mostly about Marissa, a little about science and Sean, and a tiny mention about how surprisingly cool my teachers were.

After I got home, I went straight to my room and pulled out my Chromebook to get a head start on an English assignment my teacher hadn't even assigned yet. I was that excited about blogging. When she had mentioned it in class, I raised my hand to ask, "When do we start blogging?"

An awkward pause and a couple of blank blinks later, she responded. "Well, the assignment won't be until the second quarter...but I suppose you can start it before that, if you know how."

Teachers...they were so cute. I had one word for her. "YouTube."

The rest of the class laughed, which was awesome.

So I searched YouTube for some good videos on blogging and after watching a few, I realized my biggest challenge would be deciding what to put on my blog. I knew I wanted to do both videos and write, but I wasn't sure what topics to include. Unfortunately, my life was the definition of average. Look up the definition of average in the dictionary, and it might as well read *see Kayla Burns*. I earned straight A's last year, and I knew how to surf, but that was about it. I was nothing like Aditi or Thea, who excelled at all things they tried and were two of the most motivated people I knew. They were as devoted as Alicia was with checking off items on their high achiever's to-do list.

I pulled out my sketch pad and sketched a stick figure with tight curls springing up from two high ponytails. Apparently, I was trying to draw Thea. I added a violin tucked between her waist and arm, then added all her accomplishments circling around her. Thea won violin solos in the orchestra, earned straight As, tutored her brother, helped the needy, and when she joined a club, it didn't take her too long before she led it. I did the same with Aditi, and this sketch looked more like her, probably because it was easier for me to draw her typical button up blouse and khaki pants. Aditi played the clarinet, babysat for money, wanted to organize a math club, earned straight As, and if she joined the same club Thea did, she would be the main competition for leading it. Next to Thea and Aditi, I added a terrible drawing of myself and wrote two things: straight As and surf. That was all.

There was nothing special about me.

I almost drew Marissa, but my gut clenched at the reminder of her harsh words. She abandoned us. Unlike Marissa, I was content with letting Aditi and Thea run the show.

Instead, I drew Sean, except I wrote his name in puffy letters encircled with a heart. I drew a soccer ball at his feet and tucked a surfboard under his arm. If I could draw a super cute boy, I would, but my artistic skills lacked that sort of talent.

I sighed. I kind of lacked talent in most things except reading and writing. How could I convince a cute boy like Sean to date me? Maybe that's what my blog could be about...how to be interesting.

I played around with the new blog and created a new post.

How to be Interesting

First off, let's get real. I'm boring and average. So this post is the first of many in my pursuit to become interesting. (I liked pursuit, but the phrase *become interesting* didn't work for me. I would have to fix that later.) *My besties are interesting. They excel at the violin and the clarinet, at math and science, at helping the needy and helping others. One wants to be a doctor, the other wants to be CFO of a Fortune 500 company.* [I hope this last bit means something to you. All I know (because I asked her) is that CFO stands for Chief Financial Officer.] *Even my guy friends are more interesting. One's a star soccer player who surfs, the other plays baseball and tells wicked funny jokes.*

So, for the first quarter of the school year, my personal goal is to become interesting. (Ugh, that phrase again. Can I just write *be interesting*?) *Maybe I will join a school club. Or try out for the school play. Maybe I will get better at surfing. Or maybe I will do all three. I think I need some other ideas on how to be interesting.* (Yes, be sounds so much better than become.) *Is anyone reading this? Can you give me some ideas?*

I created a generic username allowing me to use a fake name, so I signed off with *Til next time, KD.*

My last name started with a B and not a D, so I doubted anyone would recognize me. I also liked how KD sounded like Katie. I hit publish and crossed my fingers, hoping someone would respond with some advice.

But really, as I reread my post, I had to admit my ideas could work. I could join CJSF with Aditi and Thea, but I really wanted something separate from them. I knew nothing about acting, and it sounded more than a little terrifying, but maybe it was just what I needed. Of course, I could also work on my surfing, and maybe form a surf club. I knew the perfect boy to ask for help.

10: Sean

After eating tacos with my parents, I joined Jeff and Mitch and a few other guys we played with on the Xbox.

Jeff was quick to catch me up. "You just missed Mitch whining about his Xbox withdrawal."

"School was pure torture," Mitch added. "I signed in the second I got home today. Just trying to make up for all the lost time."

"Yeah, well, it was good to actually see you in real life," I said. I didn't add how pale he looked compared to Jeff and me who played sports and surfed and had lives away from the Xbox. "And it was good to see everyone else, too." I pictured Courtney and her triumphant smile when she joined her best friend in science class.

"Do you mean Kayla Burns?" Jeff asked in a teasing tone.

"Sure. Kayla and Elijah and…" I couldn't think of anyone else besides Courtney, and I wasn't about to say her name out loud.

But Jeff snorted. "Since when are you such good friends with Kayla and Elijah Jackson?"

"Since this summer?" Kayla and I hung out a lot at the surf camp, and often that sort of thing didn't transfer back to school. Kids who I thought were my friends from soccer or the neighborhood would act like they didn't know me at school. I just expected Kayla and Elijah to be like everyone else. But both clearly thought we were friends. And when it came to friends, more was always better.

"Dude," Jeff said in an all-knowing way. "Sean's going to drag us to the school dance."

It was my turn to snort. "Yeah, right. Going to a school dance is definitely on my list; right after going to a Taylor Swift concert."

While the idea of me at a school dance was ridiculous, maybe having Kayla and Elijah as friends this year would be the trick to surviving seventh grade. With one hand on the controller, I rifled through my backpack with the other until I found my notebook. I pulled it out and turned to my comic sketches. I paused in my one-handed playing to sketch out a title for my comic: Sean's Seventh Grade Survival Guide.

WANT TO READ MORE?

If you join Heather's newsletter group, you receive updates, stories, and behind-the-scenes tidbits twice a month. As a thank you for joining her list, you will also receive the downloadable prequel novella to the Surviving Seventh Grade series: *Surviving Seventh Grade: Day One.*

To learn more about Heather and her writing, visit her website authorheatherstill.com, Facebook: Heather Still Author, Instagram @stillheather4ever, Youtube@Stillpodcasts, or vist her heatherstill.substack.com. You can also learn more about the Survivng Seventh Grade series at https://www.survivingseventhgrade.com To join her newsletter list for updates, behind the scenes peeks, and free stories, sign up at https://books.survivingseventhgrade.com/ptp60eeuac

If you enjoyed the book, please consider leaving a review on Amazon or Goodreads. Thank you once again!

About the Author

Heather Still earned her Master of Fine Arts in Writing from Lindenwood University. She has taught English and history at her middle school since 2016. Her young adult writing career launched from a fabulous First Seven Sentences writing workshop by Maggie Stievater and Court Stevens that took place on Treasure Island back in 2015. Sean's Survival Guide is her debut novel in her Surviving Seventh Grade series. The second book, Kayla's Quest, will be published in April 2025.

An Excerpt from

Sean's Survival Guide

CHAPTER 1

SEVENTH GRADE SURVIVAL GUIDE TIP #1
FIND A FRIEND

If I took a scalpel to my schedule and peeled back the outer layers of teacher, subject, and classroom number, then dug around in the guts of my day, the vital organs would be friends in each class. First period pre-algebra, for instance, should have been nauseating so soon after scarfing down cereal, but the guy I sat with was cool and, more importantly, nice to me. As a bonus, one of my teammates sat on the far end, and while we couldn't work together, Elijah and I talked before and after class. Turned out math in the morning was an OK way to start my day.

Second period English found me cowering in the spotlight. I was stuck in the front, center seat, and the girl assigned to the seat behind me was almost never there. My most recent and most brutal growth spurt made it impossible to hide, so I crammed my long, skinny legs under the desk and slouched down in my seat as best I could, feeling like a resilient repellent clung to me all class. The class was pure torture.

If second period was a daily dose of dread, science class after lunch restored my will to live. I sat on the far side of class and all I had to do was sit sideways in my chair to find my best friend Jeff's smirking smile, something I did most of the time: during our teacher's lectures, during independent work, and during partner work, which kind of pissed off my partner. Not only did my best friend sit at the table behind me, but Courtney Crenshaw sat front and center. It just made sense to have good-looking students in the spotlight.

Our class was halfway through the lab prep, and my partner and I were already done—we didn't talk much. Talking slowed the process down as far as he was concerned—so I had time to kill. My partner was all about finishing early so he could do other work. I was not about to pull out work from other classes. Instead, I sat sideways in my chair to watch Jeff and his partner work through the lab prep worksheet.

"This doesn't look right," Kayla said, scrunching up her nose. She leaned over the table to peer at the worksheet. Her hair spilled forward like golden honey, the tips tapping the paper between her and Jeff. She tossed her hair back beyond a tan, bare shoulder. After a month of school, I was convinced Kayla lived in tank tops advertising surf shops.

"OK," Jeff said, matching her posture, but not her concern. Jeff wore his nonchalance like his Dodgers t-shirt, proudly for everyone to see. But when he thought no one was looking, he would do un-Jeff stuff like double check his work and frown over hard questions. Caught staring, he just shrugged at me. "Ask Sean, then."

He called me out just like that. During the beginning of sixth grade, I made the mistake of volunteering answers whenever teachers asked, and I gained an unfortunate nerd rep which had proven impossible to dodge.

"What do you think, Sean?"

I twisted farther in my seat, not sure how to respond to Kayla's question, when I accidentally made direct eye contact with her. My communication skills evaporated. After knowing Kayla Burns since kindergarten, this new-found impediment frustrated me. Her mouth saved me. She smiled her half-shy, half-mischievous smile, one that softened her features and reminded me we were something like friends last summer.

Her smile, as contagious as ever, encouraged me to risk a quick smile before I twisted the paper around to review it. "Oh, yeah. The components are wrong. It's calcium and nitrogen, not magnesium." My voice held steady, my tone too serious, but serious was my comfortable zone. "And number three needs twice the amount."

"Really? That's it?" Kayla spun the paper back around, her eyes darting from one correction to the next as if assessing my answers. "Hmm." Then her eyes slid up to meet mine. Her lips curved into another smile before she placed the back end of her pen in between her teeth. When in doubt, Kayla's go-to response was to smile. "Maybe."

My corrections were accurate, but I didn't press it for two reasons. One, Jeff didn't look like he cared either way, so I didn't want to act like I cared too much about the correct answers. Two, I wasn't sure who made the mistake in the first place and didn't want to offend Kayla in case it was her. Surviving seventh grade was eighty percent walking the social tightrope, which I figured out way too late.

Still studying the paper like it was a binding contract, Kayla flipped it over to review the answers on the back. She wasn't at all worried about caring too much. Kayla wore determination much like Jeff's nonchalance, like an accessory, obvious for all to see. She succeeded at most everything she tried, like last summer when she decided to learn how to surf and by August, she was ready to compete. There were many layers to Kayla Burns.

Her finger stabbed the paper halfway down the page as her eyes, a deep Pacific Ocean blue, met mine again. "What about this one?" Her cute smile returned.

This time I leaned over and turned the paper halfway, so then both of us could lean over it, inspecting the work as if it was important, as if grades were important, as if Jeff was the odd one out for not caring about his grade.

"It looks good," I said, but my words sounded wispy and hesitant. "Just... here." I erased half the problem and scribbled the correct answer.

On closer inspection, her eyes weren't as deep blue as the ocean because there was a heavy gray undertone that made them more earthbound, less watery. Whatever the color, the amazement in them was unmistakable.

"Wow. You make it look so easy." Another smile, this one sweeter. She had hundreds of different smiles. "Can I get your number so I can call you if I ever need help with homework?"

I blinked.

Jeff's nasally half-sneer, half-laugh could only be described as completely idiotic. "Dude," he said, "she just asked for your digits." More snickering.

An instant sunburn attacked my cheeks.

Kayla jabbed her pen into Jeff's arm. He didn't even flinch, just cocked an eyebrow my way.

"Grow up," Kayla said, turning away from him to watch my blush invade my entire face. "Seriously, though. Can I?"

I stared at the blue Bic pen she placed in my hand. Her hand rested on the edge of the table.

"Um..."

"On the top please," she said, nodding at her hand. "I don't want to risk washing it off."

"Oh, we're going old school." The words were out before I could censor them, but she giggled. I pressed the tip of the pen into the soft skin between her wrist and thumb. Halfway through inking my cell number on her hand, I snuck a quick breath. When I finished, she held her hand up in front of her face to admire my work. It was just ten digits, but she acted like I drew a cute puppy. Should I have added a puppy? Or a tagline like: *Call me!*

"Perfect," she said. "I'll add it to my phone as soon as I can."

Kayla glanced behind me towards the front of the class as if to say she was concerned about getting caught with her phone out, but our teacher was entrenched between two tables helping students. Ms. Woodson always started and ended class helping the students up front, so I wasn't sure which was more likely: Ms. Woodson catching Kayla with her phone or me catching the bubonic plague. Then again, two minutes ago I would have said the most unlikely of all was a girl asking for my phone number.

An Excerpt from Kayla's Quest

Who looks forward to returning to school after a long break?

Me! I couldn't wait to see Sean, to wish him a happy New Year with a big hug and kiss, and to walk hand-in-hand to class again. Nothing else, not seeing my friends, mattered.

Dressed in my comfy jeans and new lavender hoodie, my Vans bounced off the bleached white sidewalk with each step I took towards the main entrance to Central Valley Middle School. I might have been a tad underdressed for the chilly, gray January morning, but I had to wear my new hoodie my sister gave me for my birthday last week.

Tall palms trees flanked the school gate, swaying above the too-bright white, stucco two-story building. On the grass between the white building and the busses, the big electronic sign painted in our purple and black school colors welcomed me back with a cheery reminder that the winter dance was in a few weeks.

I breezed through the iron gate, past the sentinel palm trees, and into the front courtyard, already scanning the crowded clusters of kids for my group.

Sean and his best friend huddled in the usual spot near the math wing. Sean's light, almost blond hair stuck out on his tall, lean figure because, one: he was one of the tallest seventh graders, and two: he was one of only a few boys with naturally blond hair at my school.

I cruised around the crowded center of the courtyard by staying on the outside track.

"Hey." I grabbed his jacket and tugged him close to me. My arms snaked around his waist for a hug. "Happy New Year."

He was quick to escape my hug, but we weren't one of those annoying PDA couples. "Happy New Year, Kay. Again." He squelched any potential sting with a bright smile.

Our hands met in the open space between us. I grinned up at him. "How was the rest of your break?"

We talked and texted over break, but I only saw him in person once when he biked over to my house—which was so cool of him—but that was almost a week ago. Not seeing him for over a week was brutal.

"Break was great. I surfed and played a lot of Xbox."

"And your New Year's Eve?" I asked.

"Fine. Lots of Xbox."

Inside, I did a little victory dance. He had other options. He could have gone to her party. Best post-Christmas gift ever.

His best friend added, "I crushed him a few times on Mario Kart 3xtreme."

"And I crushed you the other ten times," Sean said in return, doing their normal boy banter thing.

I could almost forget my bestie's words of warning altogether.

As if on cue, my bestie Thea rushed over to us, the new beads from the ends of her braids clicking in a frantic rhythm. "Kayla!" Her smile threatened to bust open her face. "I did it! I won first chair!"

I squealed; she squealed. We both squealed, loud and joyous. Then came the hugs.

"Of course you got it. Congratulations, Thea!" My smile rivaled hers. "I knew you would do it. I'm so proud of you."

Whatever Thea wanted, Thea got. Not by asking for it like a spoiled rich kid, which our school had plenty, but by working her butt off to achieve it. She was my in real-life hero.

"Yeah, congratulations, Thea," Sean said. "You deserve it."

"Are you and your family going out to celebrate?" I asked Thea.

"Maybe." She shrugged, but her smile conveyed the pride and excitement she tried to downplay. She veered off to the right, waving at two kids who called out to her before waving goodbye to me. "See you at lunch!"

The warning bell thundered from the speakers overhead.

I groaned.

Sean walked me to my first period building, like he always did. We stopped off to the side when we reached the stairs to my classroom, letting classmates flow by us. We shared a quick peck on the lips. Then he waved, executed a sharp pivot in his soccer style Adidas sneakers, and walked with a confident gait back to the main part of school for his last class.

As I watched my boyfriend make his way back to the front of the school, Courtney Crenshaw and her minions stalked towards him with matching, determined sneers that I'm sure they thought counted as smiles. As always, Courtney dressed to impress, wearing skin-tight jeans, knee high leather boots, and an expensive-looking cream sweater.

Courtney's tinkling fingers did their flirty wave, which never failed to hook Sean. When the uber popular, extra venomous Courtney took time to interact with my boyfriend, he acted like putty in her hands, all too willing to be molded into whatever she wanted. He waved back, but for once, he didn't even pause in his stride. He kept walking.

Another win and school hadn't even started yet.

Seconds after I slid into the hard plastic chair of my desk, my teacher greeted the class. "Welcome back, class. I hope after the long break you all are well rested." Before the snickering and snorting got too loud, my English teacher continued, "Let's do a quick highlight share. What's one thing you want to share with the class about your break?"

The girl who sat next to me twisted around to face me and sighed dramatically. "It's that time again. What'd you do, Kayla?"

She didn't act all that jazzed about our teacher's back-from-break ritual, but my only hang up was choosing just one highlight to share. The annual Dad and Daughter Bake-off that made our entire house smell like a Christmas bakery couldn't compete with Sean's surprise visit or the epic NYE sleepover with my besties. Both were amazing! How was I supposed to choose between them?

But when the third kid shared about a sleepover, it was clear what my share needed to be. I tried to figure out the best way to explain it in as few words as possible because Ms. Ella valued being quick and concise above all else. Too soon, the boy next to me shared.

"I played Fortnite for 24 hours straight." The kids around us laughed.

Quick, just be quick. I took a quick breath, then shared in a loud, carrying voice, "My boyfriend Sean rode his bike to my house and gave me the cutest Surfing Santa snow globe."

Ms. Ella's eyebrows rose in her skeptical look she usually reserved for the annoying boys in front.

Nothing I said was offensive or *inappropriate*. Ms. Ella disliked *inappropriate* words, behavior, and topics more than she disliked rambling on aimlessly. Finally she moved on from me and allowed the next student to share.

After all thirty-three students shared, we spent twenty minutes journalling about our highlight. Even in my head the hard work at being precise for Ms. Ella was real.

I replayed Sean's visit in my head, mentally organizing the main points before I started writing.

Sean biked all the way from his house to see me on a sunny but chilly day four days after Christmas. We hung out in the family room, watching Netflix while he showed me pictures on his phone from his trip.

Ms. Ella liked lots of precise details, so I added that the smiley yellow Lau-Ipala Yellow Tang fish were my favorite. Then I added some dialogue to make it a real narrative.

"Oh," Sean said, abruptly sitting up and pocketing his phone. "I almost forgot." He grabbed his backpack from the floor and fished out a white gift bag with three triangle Christmas trees. "Here. A belated Merry Christmas...or an early happy birthday gift."

"You got me a gift?" The sweetest boyfriend ever! I pulled out the bright green, crunchy tissue paper. Detangling the heavy object from its wrapping, I giggled at the sight. "A snow globe!"

"Not just any snow globe," Sean said with his too cute grin. "A Hawaiian surfing Santa snow globe."

"It's so cute." I shook it a bunch to watch the snow flurries swirl around the Santa in his red and white board shorts. Santa looked like an expert surfer flashing a hang loose sign with his jolly grin. "I've always wanted a snow globe," I gushed. "I just never knew how cool it would be to have Santa surfing in it!" My grin was so big it could power a city.

"Right?" Sean gave me his extra sweet smile. "I saw it and knew you needed it."

I paused to flex the kinks out of my fingers. The fact Sean and I were still together after almost three months amazed me. Not too many middle school couples lasted that long. We were solid. Even with Courtney Crenshaw trying to get in the way. But just thinking of Courtney reminded me of another conversation Sean and I had during his visit.

My smile was long gone only a few words in to writing about it.

While watching Netflix, Sean asked, "Are you still going to Thea's sleepover for New Year's Eve?"

"Of course." At the time, I had smiled at the idea of spending the night with my besties but also because I loved his cute smile.

He nodded. "OK, just making sure."

But his intense look triggered an internal alarm. "Why? Aren't you and Jeff and the guys doing some Xbox marathon?"

"It's more of a tournament...but yes, that's what I'm doing." His hesitant tone made me suspicious.

"You aren't going to Courtney's New Year's Eve party, are you?"

"No..." He cleared his throat, a flush creeping up his neck. He wouldn't meet my gaze. "Probably not, I mean."

My eyes narrowed. This again. Whenever things were too good to be true, Courtney ruined it without even being there.

"And it's more a get-together than a party."

"It's still at Courtney's—" which should be a crime "—with her friends—" who were guilty of tons of social crimes at school.

Just mentioning Courtney's name turned my perfect day stormy. I wished I believed him when he said he liked me more than her. I really, really wanted to believe him. But every time I was almost there, he would say something or do something or look at her in that way of his, and doubt would win. Courtney was pretty and disgustingly popular, and worst of all, he worshipped her. How could I compete?

I grasped my pencil tight and dragged the tip across the last few lines. And then the next few lines, too. Ms. Ella didn't want to read about my stupid conversation with Sean about Courtney. I instead traced an arrow from my comment about spending NYE with my besties, past half a page of crossed out words, and then scrawled out an ending: *Right after Sean left, I searched for a good home for the gift, deciding on the bookshelf next to my Lego Wonder Woman and Invisible Jet I built last Christmas.*

"Perfect."

By lunchtime it was obvious: only super nerds like my besties were glad to be back at school. Still, I made the most out of lunch with all my friends, Sean, and his friends.

Brit, a devout gossip follower and fan of school drama, talked almost nonstop during lunch, filling us all in on all the details I didn't know I wanted to know, including updating us on Courtney's big NYE party.

"I heard only the most popular kids were there, and that she had really fancy food like chocolate fountains and stuff. Can you imagine?"

Next to me, Sean continued eating his sandwich. He glanced at me, gave a little shrug, and smiled, but he didn't say anything. But I needed to say something.

"The peperoni pizza at Thea's was so much better than a food fountain at Courtney's."

Thea snort-giggled. "Who even wants to eat food flowing from one container to another?"

"Exactly." I beamed at my best friend while Aditi and Janae giggled in agreement.

"But don't you guys wonder who was there?" Brit asked, staring right at me.

I stared right back, silently telling her to drop it. She knew Courtney had invited Sean. They all knew. But Sean didn't know my friends knew, and I didn't want to make a big deal of it! I needed to change the topic pronto.

But before I could think of what to say, Brit leaned forward again. "I wonder if Chris Thompson was there?" She sent her sly smile Aditi's way.

Oh no she didn't. Brit asked about Aditi's secret crush in front of Sean and his friends. Yes, the guys were apart of our group, but that didn't mean they got to know all of our secrets. My eyes ping-ponged between Brit's smirk and Aditi's reddening face. So not OK. But Aditi held it together. "I don' t care who was at the party."

"Me, too." I smiled at my friend.

The last thing I wanted was to tease Aditi about her ridiculous crush on Chris in front of the guys. Where she was a straight-A student, Chris prided himself on C's as if his only goal in life. Aditi wore ultra-conservative clothes like khaki pants and button up shirts with collars or polo shirts with collars, while Chris wore ripped jeans, chains, expensive looking Air Jordan's, and he even had an earring. Chris was all suave and sharp edges, sleek and powerful like a wolf. Aditi was quiet and careful, sweet and pillow soft like a bunny.

Sean ate his sandwich with a thoughtful look about him, but it was hard to tell if he was following the conversation or if he was thinking about his last soccer game. Brit tucked some hair behind one ear as she leaned forward again, her eyes still dancing with her excitement. Who knew what she was going to bring up next?

This time, I didn't hesitate. "We were at the best party of the year. And the guys did their marathon Xbox thing. Best night ever."

www.ingramcontent.com/pod-product-compliance
Lightning Source LLC
Chambersburg PA
CBHW061624130726

47996CB00003B/1114